U.B.C.
WITHDRAWN

D0578775

The
Polar Bear's Gift

Jeanne Bushey

Illustrated by Vladyana Langer Krykorka

Red Deer Press

"Please take me with you tomorrow, Ananna," Pani begged as she sat beside her grandmother on their snow sleeping bench. "I want to help you bring food into our igloo."

The woman smiled at her granddaughter. "You may come with me. You are old enough now to catch fish through the ice."

"I would rather hunt a polar bear," Pani exclaimed. "Then we would have plenty of meat for the cooking pot."

"And I would make you a new parka from its thick fur," Ananna said. Then she sighed. "It takes many men and dogs to hunt Nanook. Even then, as you know from the death of your parents, it is not easy to kill a polar bear. You and I must be content with fish and small animals."

"Someday I will hunt Nanook like my parents did," Pani declared.

"But tomorrow you will learn to fish," her grandmother said fondly.

The next morning, the sun woke Pani as it shone through the ice window of the igloo. Quickly, she pulled her worn parka over her head and hurried outside to help her grandmother harness the dogs to the sled. The team trotted swiftly across the ice until they reached the fishing place.

Pani cleared the slush from Ananna's holes with a long scoop made of caribou bone. Then her grandmother gave her a short pole. A little ivory fish hung at the end of its line.

"Jiggle the lure in the water," Ananna said. "The fish will come to see what is moving, and you will catch them."

Pani did as she was told. All at once, she felt a tug on her line. She pulled hard, and a large fish flopped onto the ice. Before long, a circle of fish lay around the hole.

Ananna was pleased when she saw the fish. She wrapped Pani's fishing line carefully around the little lure. "This was your mother's," she said. "Now it will be yours."

Pani held the ivory fish gently in her hand. "Thank-you, Ananna," she said. "I will take good care of it."

The next day, when Pani went out to play, she wore the lure in a little pouch around her neck. "Look what I have!" she called to the other children. "Yesterday I caught many fish with it. My grandmother thinks I will be a great hunter someday."

"You can't be a great hunter," a boy laughed. "Only men are great hunters!"

"Perhaps my lure is magic," Pani exclaimed.

"It doesn't look magic to me," a girl scoffed.

"It was my mother's," Pani said proudly. "She was a great hunter."

As the other children laughed, Pani put her hands over her ears and ran away.

Soon she was far out on the frozen bay. Just ahead, a pale shape lay on the ice. "Perhaps it is Netsirq sunning himself beside his breathing hole," Pani thought. "If I had a harpoon, I could bring fresh seal meat to Ananna. Then no one would laugh at me."

But as she went closer, Pani saw the animal was not a harmless seal. It was a young polar bear! Quickly, she looked around. If a cub was asleep on the ice, his mother was probably not far away.

Pani knew she should run back and bring the hunters to track the mother bear. She peered at the cub as it lay motionless on the snow. Suddenly, she had an idea. "If the cub is dead instead of asleep, I could bring it back to the village, and everyone would think I killed it myself."

Cautiously, Pani crept closer. Sure enough, there was a deep wound in the cub's side. Had he been bitten by a hunter's dog and crawled here to die? Pani bent over the cub. Dark blood caked his white fur and oozed from the injury. As her hand touched his side, he opened his eyes and growled in pain!

Pani backed away, her heart beating wildly. The bear might not
be dead yet, but he soon would be. All she had to do was wait.
Pani looked at the cub, and he stared back at her. Then his
dark eyes closed in pain. The girl thought how
happy Ananna would be when she
returned with the dead bear.

Minutes passed. Then,
weakly, the bear's eyes
opened again and looked
at Pani. She could almost
hear him asking for help.
With a sigh, she made up
her mind. "It's all right,
Nanook," she said. "I will
take care of you."

Pani scooped some snow into her mouth and held it until it melted. She squirted the warm water onto the bloody wound. It took many mouthfuls of water, but finally she was satisfied that the injury was clean. "Now he needs some food," Pani said to herself.

There was a deep crack in the ice not far from where the bear lay. Pani took her fishing line from its pouch. She dropped the ivory lure into the crack and jiggled it up and down just as Ananna had taught her. In less than a minute, a fish struck.

"I knew my mother's lure was magic!" Pani exclaimed.

At first the bear only nibbled the fish. Then he ate faster and faster. As soon as he had eaten one fish, Pani caught him another. At last the bear struggled to his feet.

"Thank-you for saving my life," he said in a deep voice. "My mother will want to thank you, too. Please come with me to my igloo."

Pani had heard many stories about animals who could talk, so she followed the little bear across the ice. However when they arrived at the bear's igloo, she was frightened and hid behind the cub.

The mother bear was waiting anxiously for her son's return. "Where have you been?" Mother Bear growled. "I looked everywhere for you. I was sure you were bitten by the hunter's dogs." Suddenly, she spotted Pani. She stood up on her hind legs and growled fiercely. "Who is this person you have brought to our igloo?"

Quickly, the little bear showed his
mother the wound in his side. He told
her how Pani had saved his life.

Mother Bear looked at Pani. "You could have let my son die and taken his fur and meat to your village," she said in a soft voice. "Only a great hunter would have shown such kindness." She handed Pani a small white bag. "The pieces of fur in this bag are magic. Use them, and you will never be hungry or cold again."

Pani thanked the mother bear, and the little bear led her back to her village.

"Good-bye, Nanook. I will never forget you."

"Perhaps we will meet again some day," the little cub replied.

Pani crawled into her igloo and told her grandmother everything that had happened. "Here is the bag Mother Bear gave me," she said.

Ananna took a small piece of fur out of the bag. At once, it grew until it covered the whole floor of the igloo!

"This is enough to make you a new parka and pants as well," Ananna gasped. Then she threw a second piece of the magic fur into the cooking pot and sat down to sew. By the time the bubbling stew was ready to eat, Pani's clothing was finished.

"The polar bear's gift is magic indeed!" Ananna exclaimed. "We must invite everyone to share in our feast."

From that day on, the polar bear's bag was never empty, and Pani and her grandmother enjoyed good fortune for the rest of their lives.

Text Copyright © 2000 Jeanne Bushey
Illustrations Copyright © 2000 Vladyana Langer Krykorka
Published in the United States in 2001

All rights reserved. No part of this publication may be reproduced, stored in a retrieval system or transmitted, in
any form or by any means, without the prior written permission of Red Deer Press or, in case of photocopying or
other reprographic copying, a licence from CANCOPY (Canadian Copyright Licensing Agency), 1 Yonge St., Suite 1900,
Toronto, ON M5E 1E5, FAX (416) 868-1621.

Northern Lights Books for Children are published by
Red Deer Press
56 Avenue & 32 Street Box 5005
Red Deer Alberta Canada T4N 5H5

Credits
Edited for the Press by Peter Carver
Cover and text design by Blair Kerrigan/Glyphics, and Vladyana Langer Krykorka
Printed in Hong Kong for Red Deer Press

Acknowledgments
Financial support provided by the Canada Council, the Department of Canadian Heritage and the Alberta
Foundation for the Arts, a beneficiary of the Lottery Fund of the Government of Alberta.

THE CANADA COUNCIL | LE CONSEIL DES ARTS
FOR THE ARTS | DU CANADA
SINCE 1957 | DEPUIS 1957

COMMITTED TO THE DEVELOPMENT OF CULTURE AND THE ARTS

Canadian Cataloguing in Publication Data
Bushey, Jeanne, 1944–
The polar bear's gift
(Northern lights books for children)
ISBN 0-88995-220-5
1. Inuit – Canada – Juvenile fiction. 2. Polar bear – Juvenile fiction.
I. Krykorka, Vladyana. II. Title. III. Series.
PS8553.U69654P64 2000   jC813'.54   C00-910481-X
PZ7.B96546Po 2000

5 4 3 2 1

For Kyra, her mommy, Sarah, and her auntie, Jessie
– Jeanne Bushey

To Michael Arvaarluk, my Arctic inspiration
– Vladyana Langer Krykorka

2411333

PZ7.B96546

ok cur